UNICORN'S TOOLS
KEEP OUT!

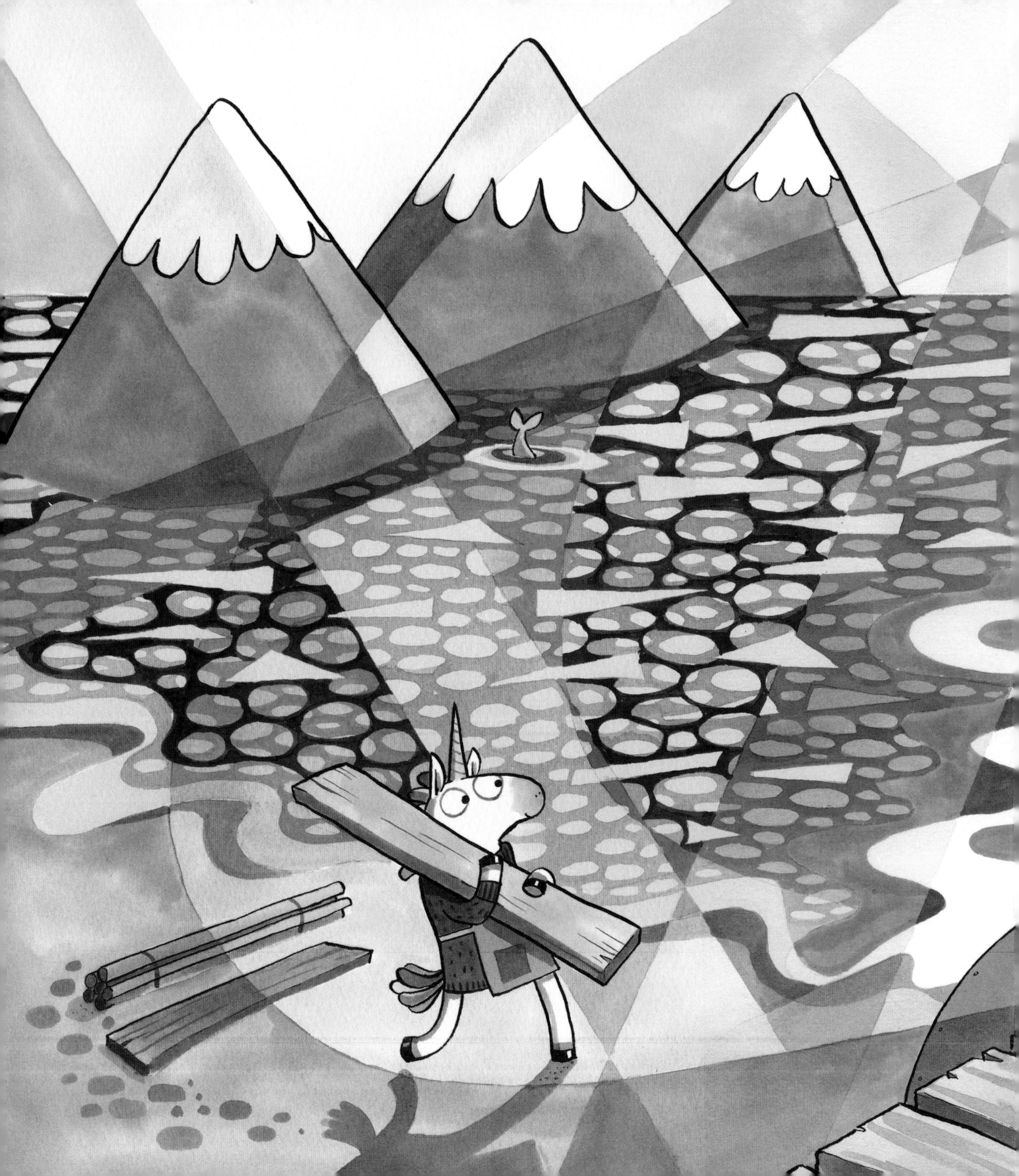

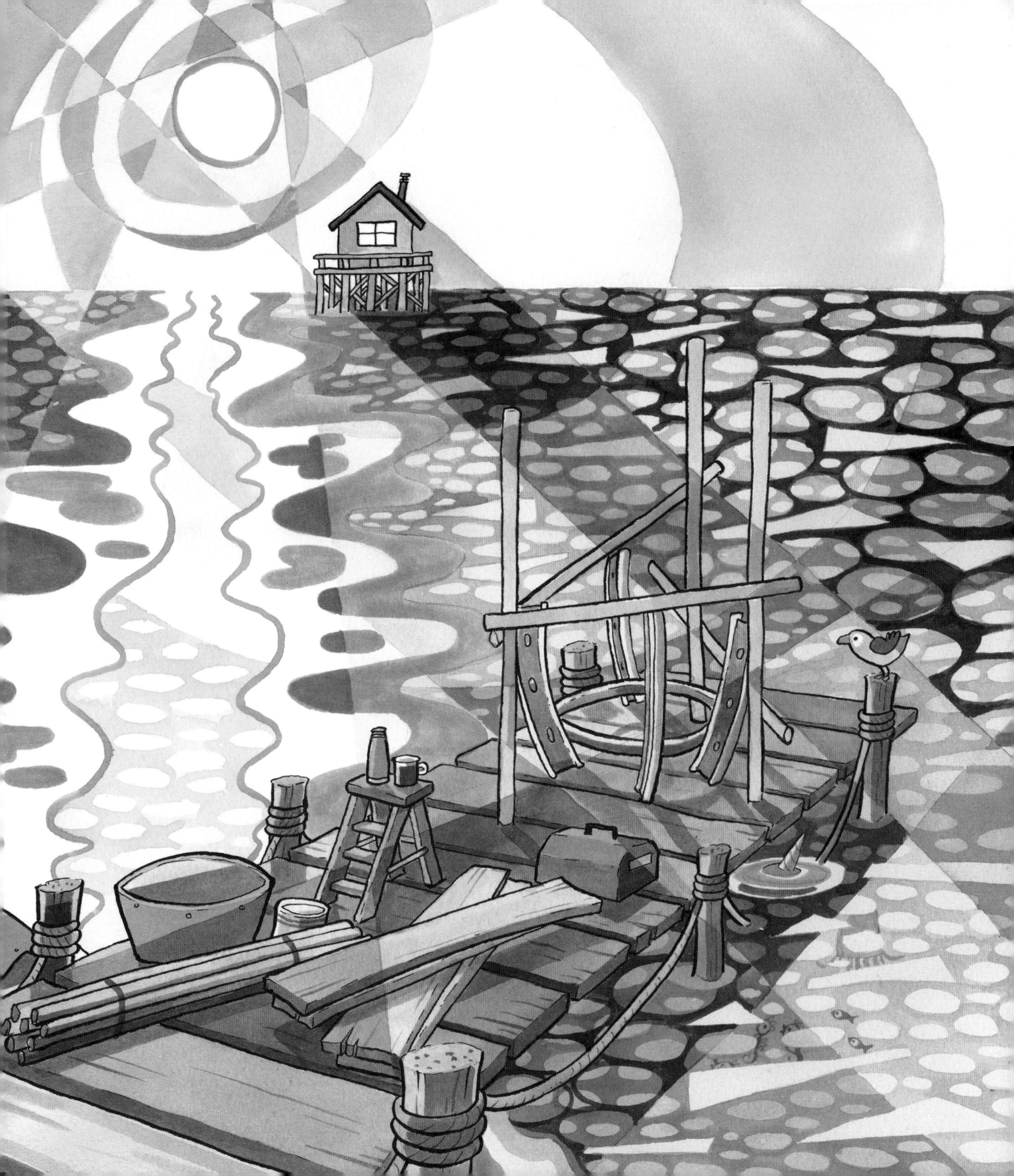

FOR MY SISTER JOYCE LEE

First published in 2020 by Scholastic Children's Books,
a division of Scholastic Ltd.
No 1 London Bridge,
London SE1 9BG
All rights reserved. Published by Scholastic Inc., *Publishers since 1920.*
SCHOLASTIC and associated logos are trademarks and/or registered
trademarks of Scholastic Inc.

Library of Congress Cataloging-in-Publication Data Available

ISBN 978-1-338-82871-9

10 9 8 7 6 5 4 3 2 1   23 24 25 26 27

Printed in the U.S.A. 76
First American edition, July 2023

Don't Call Me Grumpycorn

By Sarah McIntyre

Scholastic Inc.

Unicorn was sitting in his brand-new rocket.

"I'm going to visit the most **fabulous** planet in the universe," he said.

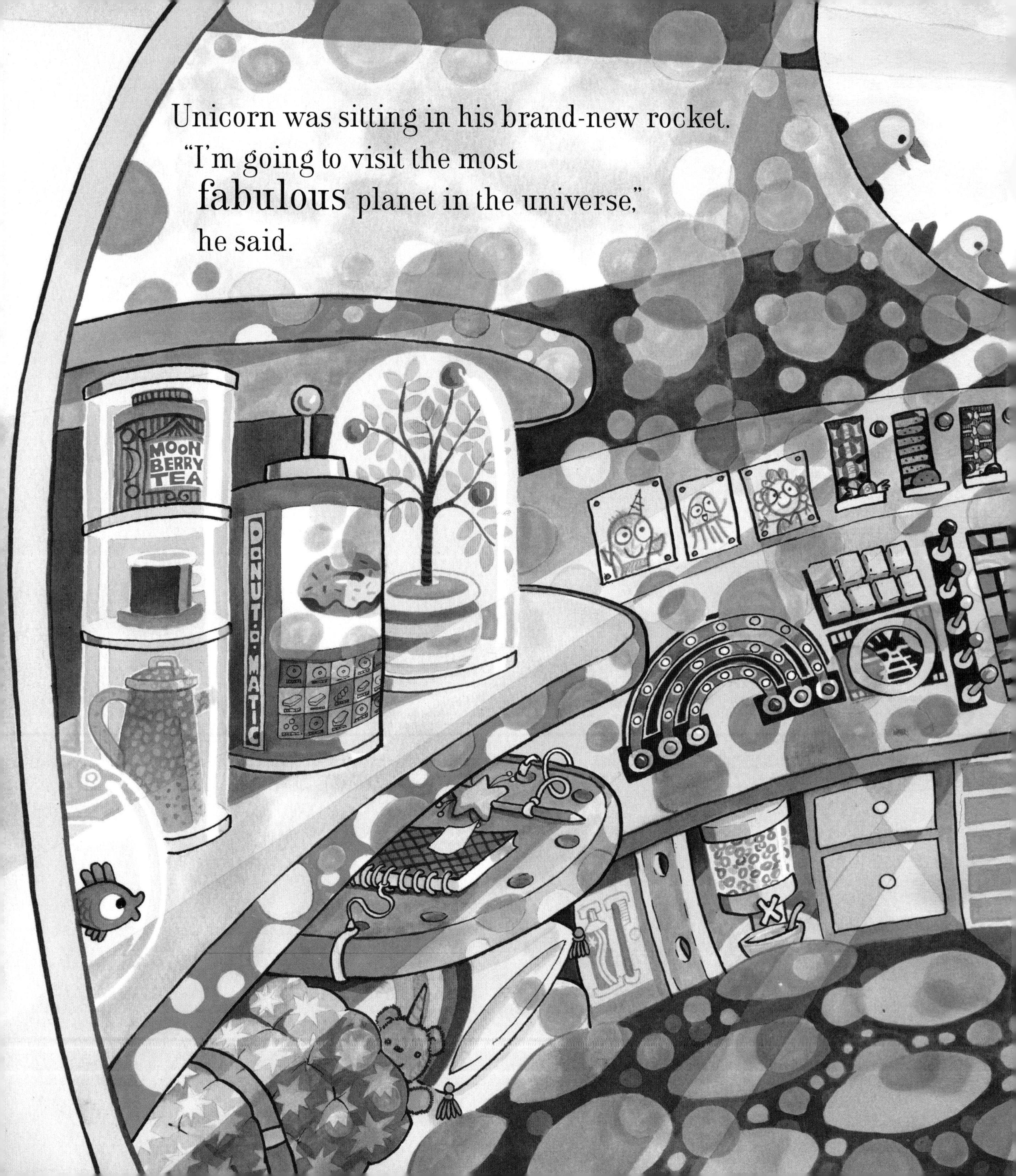
MOON BERRY TEA
DONUT-O-MATIC

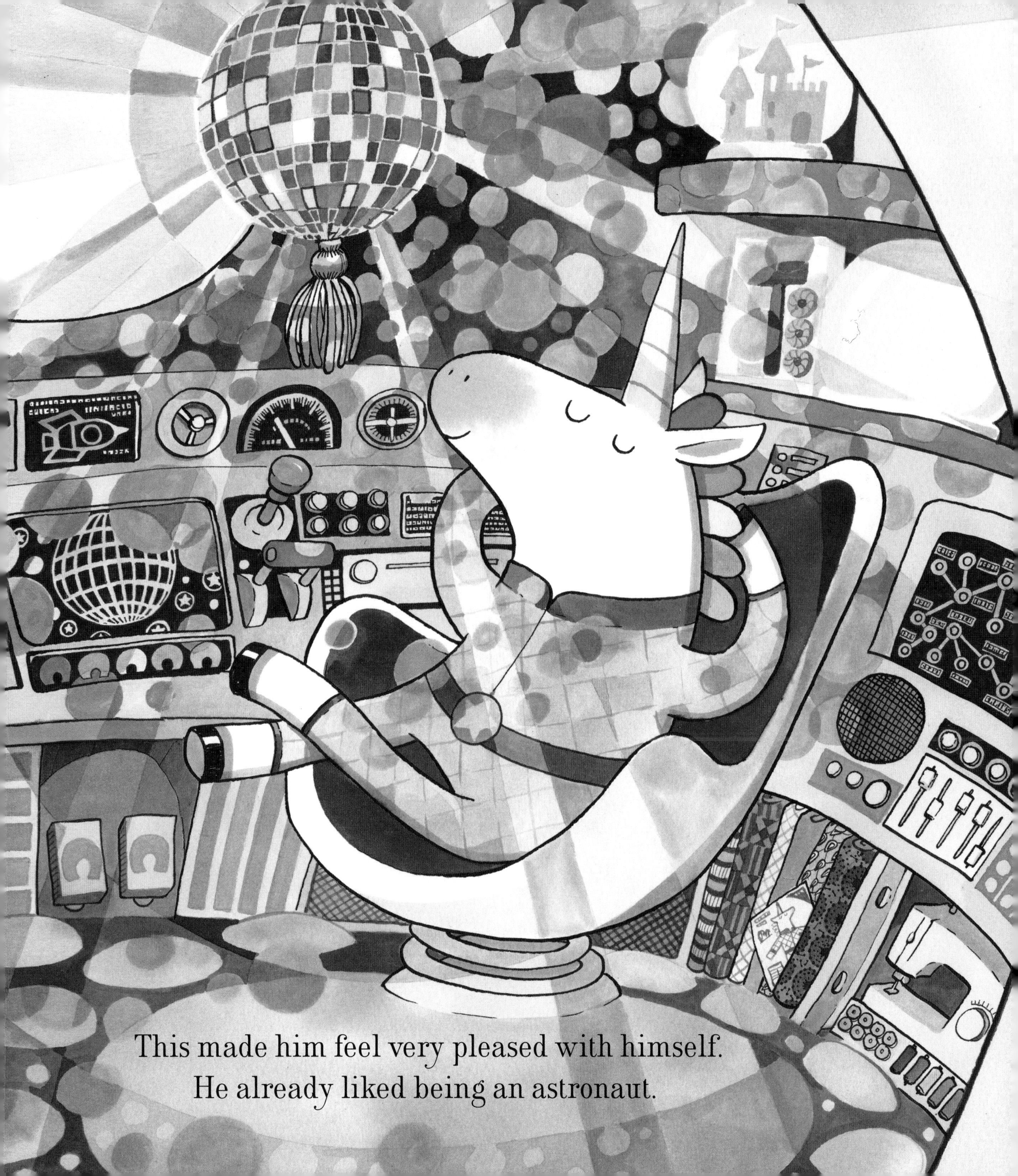

This made him feel very pleased with himself.
He already liked being an astronaut.

"Wait for me!" called out a voice.
It was Mermaid.

"Can I come, too?" she asked.

"But there are no mermaid astronauts,"
said Unicorn.

"But there COULD be," said Mermaid.
"Floating in space will be just
like floating in the sea."

When Unicorn turned around,
he saw that his other friends,
Narwhal and Jellyfish, were
already in the rocket.

Unicorn sighed. "All right. You can all go into space with me. But only if you let me be the FIRST to walk on the planet."

Secretly, he was a little bit happy. He had been nervous about going into space all by himself.

Jellyfish asked, "Can I do the countdown?"

"Only if you let me say 'BLAST OFF'!" said Unicorn.

Jellyfish counted.

10 9 8 7 6 5 4 3 2 1

They all waited.

Narwhal whispered, "Aren't you supposed to say 'BLAST OFF'?"

"I was waiting to make it extra **fabulous**," said Unicorn.

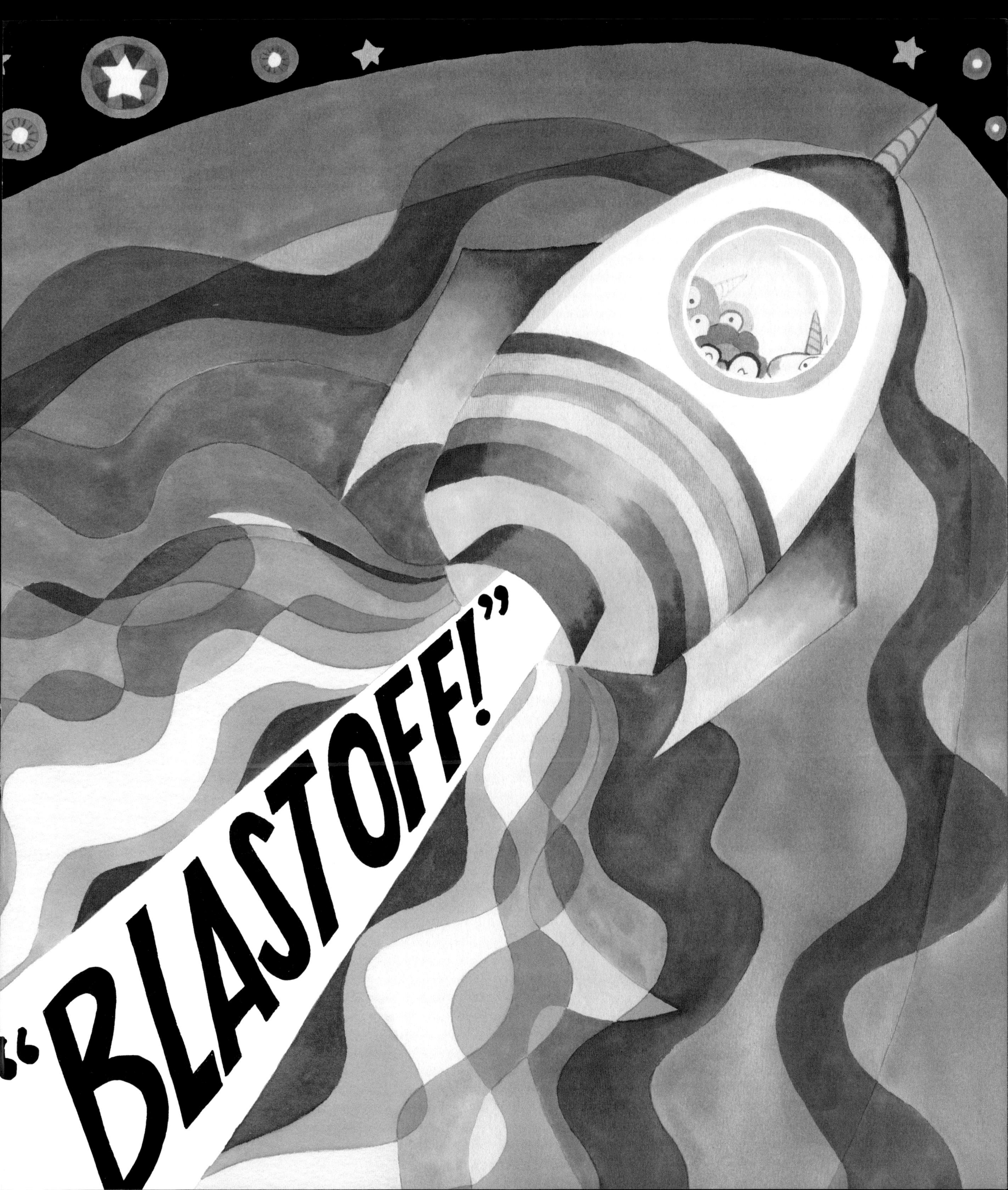
"BLASTOFF!"

Mermaid said,
"Look at me! I'm floating!"

"Whee!" said Narwhal.
Jellyfish giggled so hard,
she got the hiccups.

"HIC! HIC!"

"Ooooh," said Mermaid.
"Why don't we visit that planet?
I think I see some alien mermaids!"
"No," said Unicorn. "That planet does not
look fabulous enough. Let's keep going."

"Can we stop at this planet?" asked Narwhal. "What a beautiful planet!"

"No," said Unicorn. "Let ME choose— going into space was MY idea."

"This is the BEST planet... **HIC!**" hiccuped Jellyfish. "Surely we can stop here."

"No!" snapped Unicorn. "Would you all be quiet and let me fly the rocket? You are all back-seat astronauts and I am VERY ANNOYED!"

"What a Grumpycorn!" said Jellyfish.

"DON'T CALL ME GRUMPYCORN!" hollered Unicorn. "Call me...CAPTAIN."

"Captain Grumpycorn," giggled Jellyfish.

"**HIC!**"

Their rocket touched down neatly on a sparkly purple planet.

Everyone put on their spacesuits and got stuck in the doorway as they all tried to go out at once.

"NO!" said Unicorn. "It must be ME who goes out the door first. ME!"

Unicorn made a grand entrance onto the fabulous planet and planted his unicorn flag in the grass.

"That's one small step for a unicorn, and one giant leap for unicorn-kind!"

"Except we've never met another unicorn," said Mermaid. "So it is just a giant leap for you."

"**HIC!**" said Jellyfish.

"This planet is SO fabulous that surely
there will be more unicorns here," said Unicorn.
"What more could anyone want?"
"I could want to get rid of my hiccups," said Jellyfish.
Just then, Jellyfish gave a surprised hiccup. "HIC!"
Mermaid whispered, "We are surrounded!"

"Are these unicorns fabulously friendly?" asked Narwhal.
"My new fabulous friends!" whinnied Unicorn. He ran off to play with them.

Narwhal, Mermaid, and Jellyfish waited for Unicorn to come back to them. They waited and waited. Mermaid asked, "How will we know which one is **our** unicorn?"

"I do not know," said Jellyfish. "How can we make him come back?" She gave a nervous giggle. "HIC!"

They were very loud hiccups. "HIC!"

Unicorn was not sure he liked being around all these fabulous unicorns. All the unicorns were busy doing fabulous things…

but he felt a little bit lost.

"HIC!"

"What is that annoying sound?"
asked the unicorns.
"Make it go away."

"HIC!"

said
Jellyfish.

The unicorns herded Mermaid, Narwhal, and Jellyfish
back into the rocket.
"Goodbye," they said. "We only want fabulous unicorns on this planet."

The three friends sat
in the rocket.

"**HIC!**" said Jellyfish very quietly.
"I suppose I will go find the
mermaid planet," said Mermaid.
"And I will find the narwhal
planet," said Narwhal.
"I don't want to go to
the jellyfish planet,"
said Jellyfish.
"I want to go home."

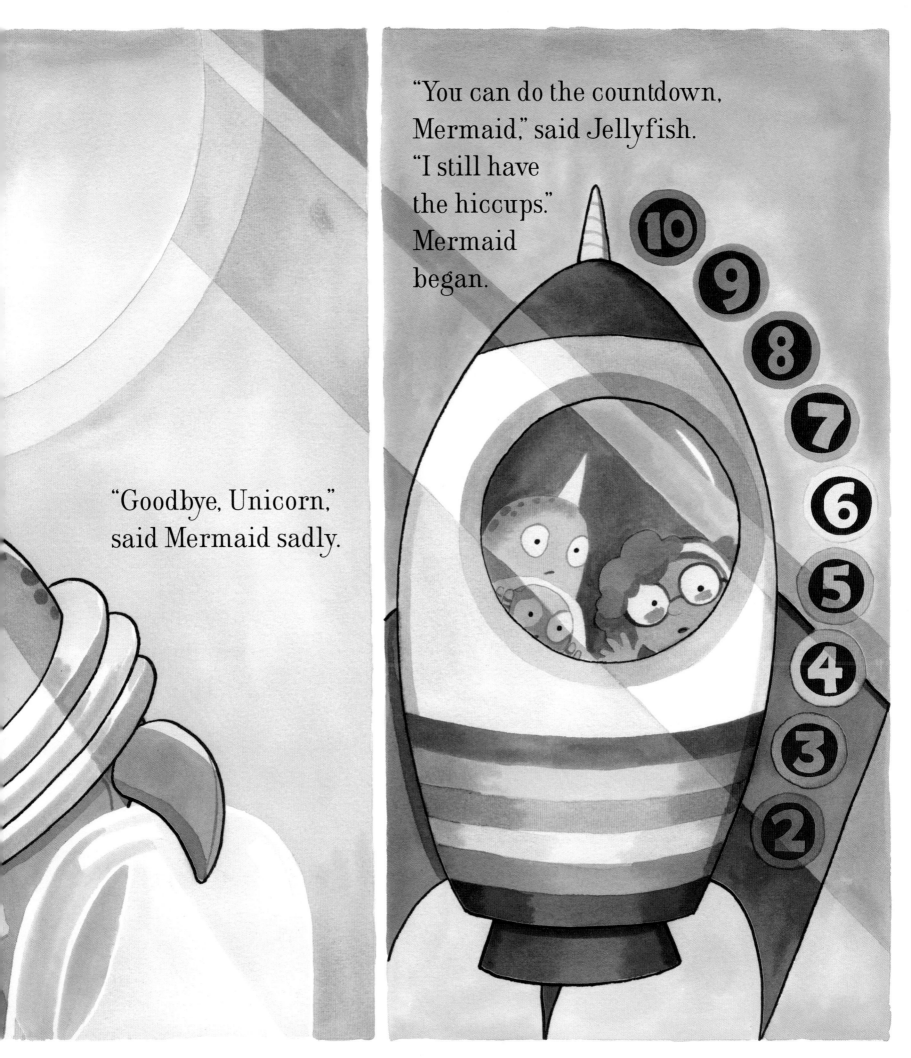

"Goodbye, Unicorn," said Mermaid sadly.

"You can do the countdown, Mermaid," said Jellyfish. "I still have the hiccups." Mermaid began.

"WAIT!"

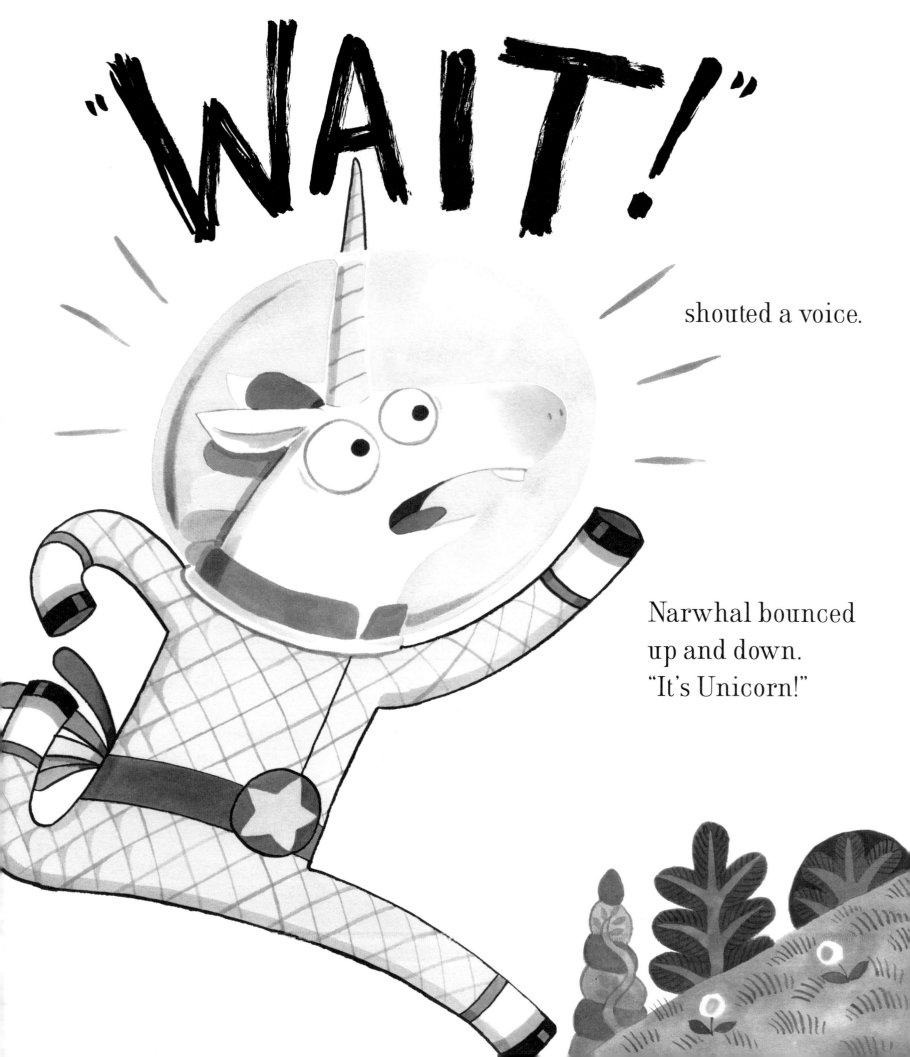

shouted a voice.

Narwhal bounced
up and down.
"It's Unicorn!"

"Please don't leave without me!" panted Unicorn.

"But don't you want to stay with all the other fabulous unicorns on the most fabulous planet in the universe?" asked Mermaid.

"HIC!"
said Jellyfish.

"No," said Unicorn. "They were not very fabulous because they were not very kind to you. I was not very kind to you, either. I would rather go to a planet where all four of us can live together."

Jellyfish wriggled with happiness. "I'm so glad...that my hiccups have stopped!"

"Let's go back to our own fabulous planet,"
said Narwhal.

So they did.

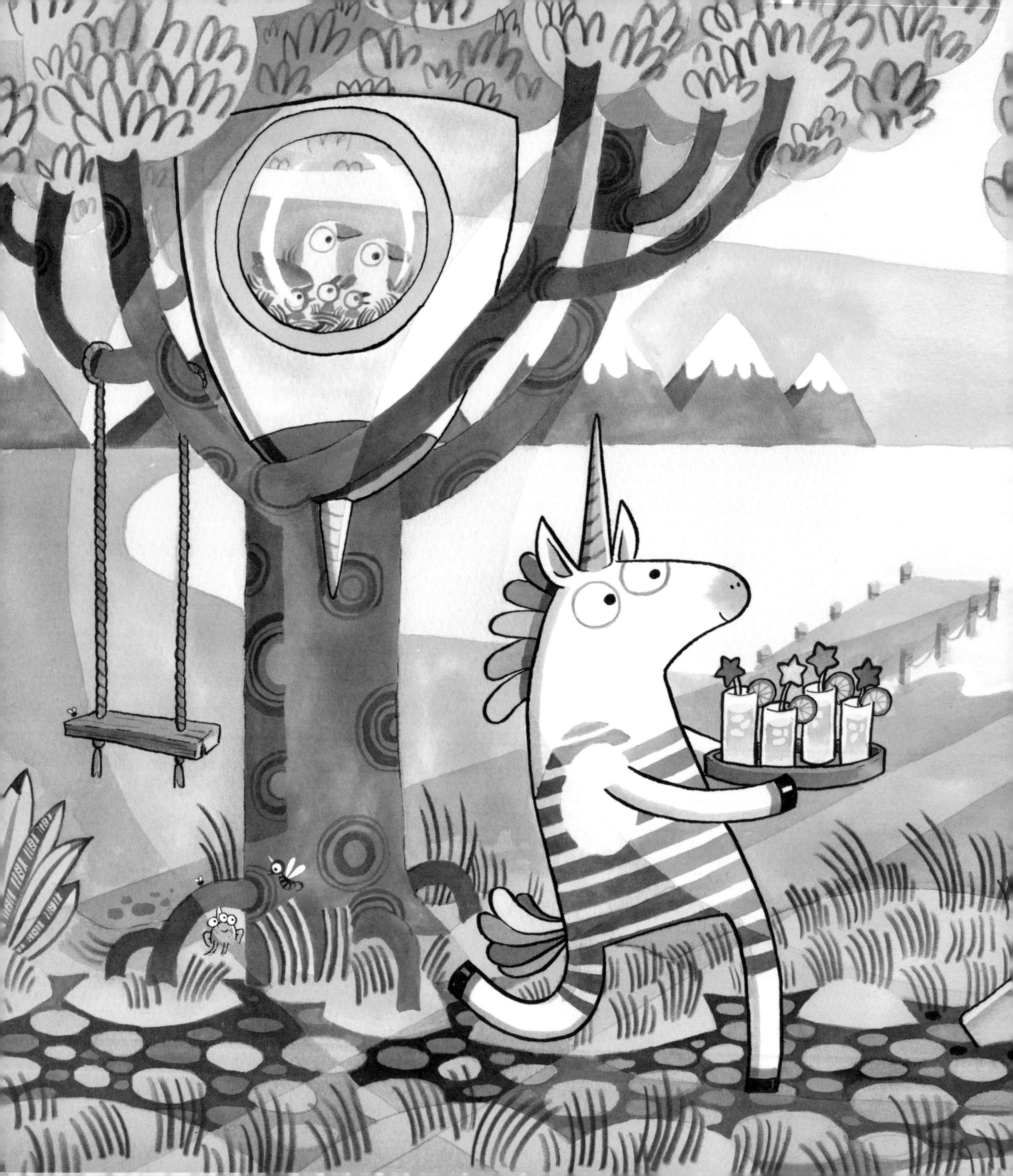

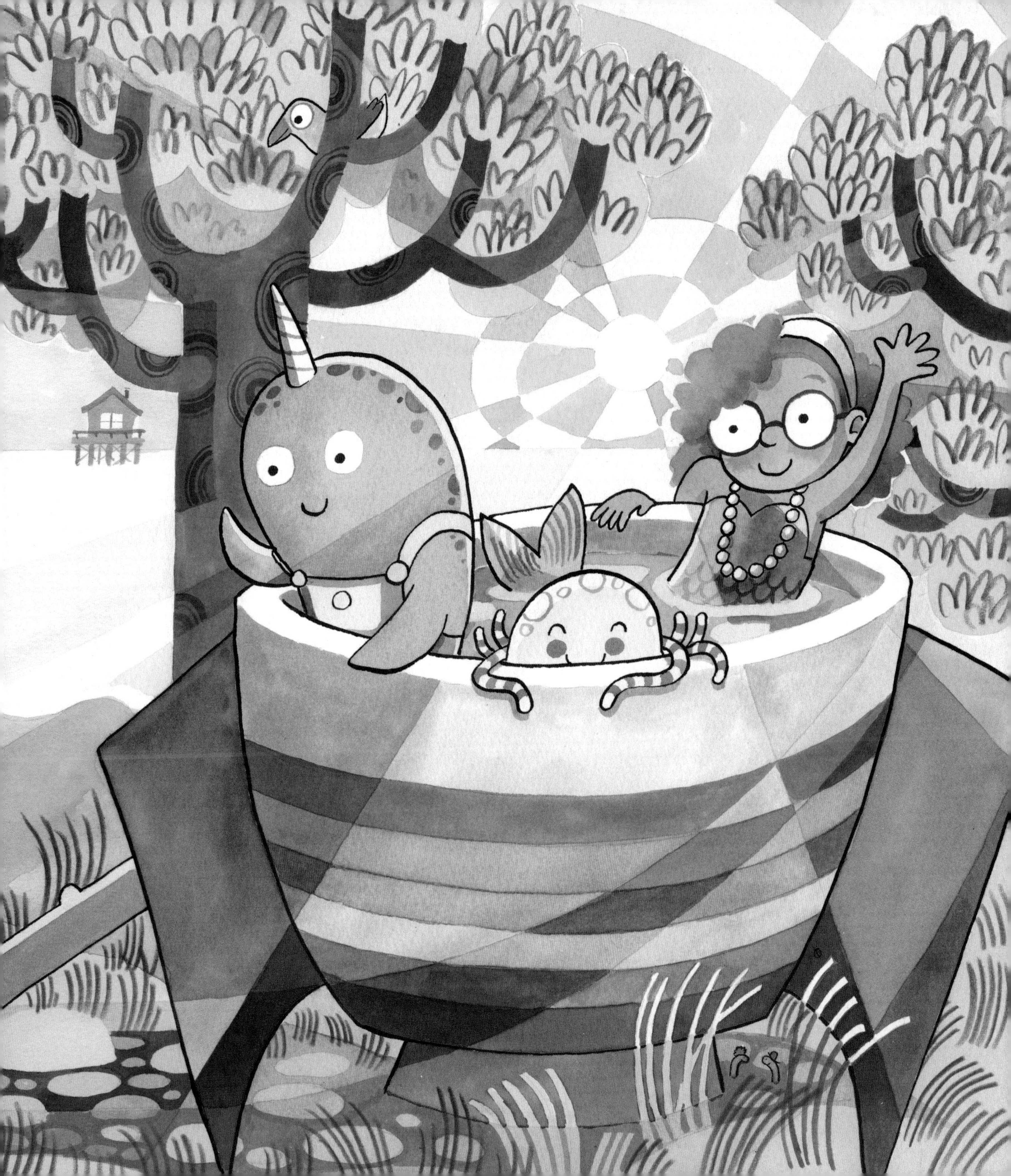